C000255678

CHAPTER 1

ZARAH

he sound of mandolins in the piazza, a spoonful of limone gelato melting on my tongue, and the ass-kicking beauty of an Italian afternoon. *La dolce vita.* It is one hell of a sweet life. A golden glow has settled over the entire scene, making me feel as if I'm part of a Renaissance painter's master-piece. I'm the contented woman in the foreground. At thirty-four, the smile I wear is genuine and my sigh an exclamation point.

My month in Italy is coming to an end. There are just three more days to soak it all in before heading back to Manhattan. This trip has been exceptional, and it was more than the hidden beach I found, or the breathtaking zip lining experience in the Alps. As usual, I found God in the details. The food and wine, the play of light moving across ancient stone buildings. It was in the laughter and conversations shared with friends.

Outdoor cafes like this one are the first thing I look for in a city. They give me a chance to observe and take notes for my travel blog while indulging in the local fare. Other times I make small talk with fellow tourists. I don't really care that today the German couple at the table to my right are watching me. They think they're being clever—faces forward eyes to the side. But I catch the stares. It may be my loud sighing or possibly the spiked white hair.

Going prematurely gray at nineteen had its challenges. Now I understand looking this way isn't necessarily a bad thing. It reflects who I am at the core, a woman made different. I'm a loner and a wanderer who's not afraid of much. I'll jump out of a plane or eat disgusting looking insects if they're the delicacy. There's been a few times I hesitated, but not once have I regretted embracing the unknown. It's good not to be aware of what pleasures the day will bring.

I travel the world free of companions. A happy adventurer. Sort of a one-woman band who takes comfort in her own company. Not to say I refuse an erotic romp or week-long affair when it interests me. Shit, I'm only human. Sometimes those are the most interesting journeys of all. And in between my travels I reboot myself in my tiny apartment in New York with a small circle of close friends. Well, mostly it's me and my BFF, Stori.

Kicking off my sneakers, I stretch my bare legs then bring them up atop the iron chair across from me. Lavender-painted toes wiggle and widen. My attention is drawn to the couple who just sat down a few minutes ago at the other end of the café. That's not completely accurate because they're arguing and one of the two of them is always standing. They're taking turns threatening to leave. I don't have to be fluent in the language to get the picture.

First, the woman refuses to sit. She tosses long dark hair over her shoulder and gives him a piercing look with eyes ablaze. Then, when he convinces her to stay, she says one word, and he stands and throws his napkin on the table. Both Italian born I'd say. His hands are raising and gesturing dramatically. The fingers of her right hand are pulled together and held up in front of him to emphasize just how pissed she is. It's fucking funny.

Reminds me of a bad movie where both costars are overacting. I can't see the guy's face, but the back of him is worthy of admiration. An ass I could bounce quarters off, thick head of hair, muscles developed by obviously consistent workouts. Great-fitting clothes. Yummy yum yum. I'll add one more yum to that assessment. He could look like Frankenstein from the front, but this view does the man justice.

Suddenly the woman looks at the tables next to theirs, scanning for something. Only she knows what. Without a word she picks up a half-finished glass of red wine from the shocked woman it belongs to and throws it on the sexy Italian's crotch. By his reaction he didn't see it coming. His hands lift in the air as he looks down at his expensive, perfectly tailored stained pants.

This would be a great photograph. *Italian Saturday* captured in a telling frozen moment. I grab my cell and become the photographer. The twenty or so customers at the café are shocked at first. Then it turns into amusement. I'm chuckling too.

In all my travels I've never known a culture so passionate. They're vocal and demonstrative in their love. Doesn't matter who sees it either. Tears and arguments are both expected, accepted and part of the romance. *Oh! That'll be my slant on the blog next month!*

The click click clicking of the woman's heels walking away and the pinched look on her face ends their conversation. The man takes his napkin and dabs the front of his pants.

I'm not sure these two were destined for more. But sometimes the draw of a pretty face, or strong arms, or an exceptional cock makes a compelling argument. You stay together because of the visual. Everyone says you look great together. It's a rookie mistake, forgivable only in the young. If you stay with someone solely for their looks after you've passed thirty, you're a dick. Male or female.

The man turns around and puts an abrupt end to my fantasies. As soon as I see the face, I know exactly who it is. A feeling of happiness bubbles up inside me. Holy shit, I'm sixteen again! But now I'm looking at a grown man. A handsome one.

"Fig!" I stand and call across the tables. "Figaro!" I wave.

His eyes search the tables, looking for a familiar face. They settle on me. Brows knit together and his head tilts. It takes him a moment to put it all together, but when he does a crooked smile lifts the corner of his mouth. My arms open wide and my fingers wiggle, calling him to me.

He lifts one finger, asking for my patience. Taking out some cash he places it under the edge of the napkin of the woman whose wine was thrown. He says something to her and extends his hand. She accepts and nods her thank you.

As he comes toward me, arms open like mine, he's laughing. He dips his head and nibbles on his bottom lip. Damn. Can he be any sexier?

"Zarah! You're like a mirage in the desert. Come here!" he says taking me in his awesome arms and not letting go.

I feel enveloped in affection. It's sincere and welcoming. And man, he smells great. What is that cologne? Fuck Me Now, by Dolce and Gabbana? When we part I feel his biceps.

"Wow! Those are new," I say.

He's a bit embarrassed. I recognize the shyness that I knew in school. He was always the quiet Dragoni twin. But the sensual Italian accent never failed to dazzle me. Even when we were freshmen in high school and his voice was made of changing octaves.

Now a soft-spoken, deep tone has replaced it. Unexpectedly, he takes my face in his hands and kisses me right on the lips. I know it's just a friendly gesture, but I can't help but notice they're soft, luscious and every other adjective that means the same.

"I always wanted to do that," he says. "Thank you for giving me an excuse."

"Well, don't keep me in suspense. Was it good for you?"

"Of course. Just as I suspected," he says, eyes twinkling.

I throw my arms around his neck and return the kiss, making sure to give it my best. It surprises the hell out of him.

"I agree. Just as suspected," I say.

He looks deeply into my eyes and nods his head in amazement.

"It's been seventeen years, Zarah. I can't believe you're here. Are you in Italy by yourself? Or maybe with your husband?"

"I'm single. And here for three more days, anyway."

"Good. Let's visit. I want to know everything," he says.

He holds out a chair for me to sit, and when I do, he makes sure to push it in till I'm comfortable. It doesn't escape me that I'm not looking my best. Shorts, discarded sneakers, Stones vintage T-shirt. So generic. And I've got that stupid Batman band aid on where I scraped my leg. Crap.

He comes around and sits across from me. Leaning in he takes my hands in his. "I'm so happy to see you again," he says softly.

How is it I forgot about his hazel eyes? They're not only gorgeous, but kind. They radiate a soulful quality. Somehow, I didn't notice back then. As stupid as it sounds it could have happened. I was more popular with the girls than the boys in high school, and my exposure to them was limited. Plus, I put some off with my do-anything say-anything personality.

"I'm surprised you even remember me, Fig. I hadn't gone gray yet then, so I know it's not the hair."

"It's great by the way. Very chic. And you're kidding about remembering you, right? I had a crush on you, bella."

"What?" I think my mouth must have just dropped open.

"You didn't know? Come on."

I would say he's kidding, but by the serious look on his face I know I'd be wrong.

"I was never the girl boys were interested in. I was a flat chested, braces wearing loner."

"That's not what I saw," he says locking eyes with me.

"Really?"

"I saw a delicate girl with dark green eyes that have golden flecks in them. And she had the most delightful laugh."

Am I blushing? It sure feels like it, as unfamiliar as the event is.

"I never knew."

"Plus the fact you'd say the word fuck every so often, no matter who heard. I thought you weren't afraid of anything."

"I always had a sailor's mouth."

"It was charming to me."

Luckily my embarrassment is interrupted by the young white-aproned server offering us menus.

"No, no. No need for menus," Fig says turning to me. "Shall we enjoy a little wine?"

"Definitely."

"Vino Brunello, per favore."

He nods to the server and as the man walks away, Fig leans back in his chair and just grins at me.

"What?" I say.

"You've completely turned my day."

I pitch my thumb in the direction his last companion went. "If I can ask, what was that about? It was very entertaining."

He shakes his head. "I'm embarrassed. It's not like me at all. Really, don't judge me because of what you saw. That woman didn't take what I had to tell her well."

"Then she's the injured party?" I say.

He thinks for a moment about how he's going to respond. "She shouldn't be. We only went out once. She had ideas." He makes a circling gesture to the side of his head. "We weren't compatible in any way."

"She was stunning."

"Was she?" he says with a lopsided grin.

The way he's looking at me is making the back of my neck hot. Not to mention my southern territories.

"So you're living back in Italy now?" I say, changing the subject.

"No. I'm here for a friend's wedding. And to visit the familia. I've been living in New York for two years."

"I'm still a New Yorker too! Whenever I'm not traveling. I have a travel blog, Zarah's Way."

"How wonderful. You were always interested in seeing other countries. And you were independent. Even at fourteen. I remember," he says tapping his temple.

As the waiter reappears and uncorks the bottle, Fig tells me his story. What came after our years together at Mater Dei High School. How the Dragoni Tire Company grew to be a worldwide brand, and how Fig and his brother Luca have worked in the family business for over a decade now. He for the last few years in New York and Luca in Italy.

I'm listening to every word, but something deep inside me is focused on the silent conversation we're having. The one made entirely of subtext. The look in his eyes, the smile on my lips, the occasional touch of our hands. And above all the za za zing that's passing between us.

"My God. I've taken over the entire conversation. Blah, blah, blah. I'm boring you for sure," he says in that adorable accent.

I think he's nervous. Awesome!

"Of course you're not boring me! It's gonna take us at least three more long conversations to catch up. Don't you think?" I say.

"At least three. Maybe more. And while we do that we might as well catch a few sights. Maybe I could take you to some of my favorite places around Positano and Rome. We could put your last few days to good use…you know, for your blog," he says, eyes twinkling.

We stare at each other for a good five seconds before I respond.

"And I could show you a few of my personal favorites that I bet would surprise you. Places so exquisite and hidden they would take your breath away," I volley.

He takes a few beats before he answers. "You've already done that, bellezza."

CHAPTER 2

FIG

"How does she look?" Luca says over the taunting background laughter of my six-year-old niece and the piercing screams of her little brother. Even through the phone they sound as if they're right next to me.

"Bellissimo. She's very attractive. What are you doing, beating your children again?"

He goes into a fifteen second Italian lecture at the top of his lungs that neither child is listening to. And he ends it with an English warning. "I'm sending your mother in if you don't stop hitting each other!"

"That's it, threaten them with your wife." I laugh.

"You know she'd take charge. Bring Zarah over. We can go out for dinner. Caroline would love to see her again."

I stop him there. "Thanks, But no. We're going exploring for a few days."

"What? You're kidding me."

"Not in the least. I need you to do me a few favors."

"Sure."

"Let Mom and Dad know I'm going out of town and I'll call in a few days. I'll be talking with Nona myself. And I was going to meet with my former staff for lunch on Thursday. Tell them I'm sorry, but something came up. No, tell them I'm sick, whatever. Get me out of it."

"Can I tell them your dick came up and cancelled all your appointments without your permission?"

"No. Please don't do that, Luca."

He just chuckles. I wouldn't put it past him. He's the wildcard of our family.

"When are you leaving for the wedding?" he says.

"Friday."

"You taking her?"

"No. I don't know. Maybe."

He let's out a long whistle followed by, "Oh, brother!"

I imagine his head shaking.

"What?" I say.

"This isn't like you. None of this. The impulsive decision to travel with someone you really don't know, the cancellation of the lunch, the idea you may be bringing her to a place that means so much to you. It sounds much more like something I would have done. You're the predictable one."

It kinda pisses me off to have to explain myself.

"First of all, I do know her. If you remember she was in our close circle of friends in high school. Secondly, I'm canceling a lunch? Big deal. Thirdly, go fuck yourself, Luca. Just do as I ask. Please."

"Alright, alright. Go play with your sexy classmate."

"Who are you talking about?" I hear Caroline's voice, and Luca's sudden change in tone.

"I'm talking to Fig about Zarah. He ran into her."

I can picture Caroline now. She's gone silent with jealousy, punishing Luca for being himself and using the word sexy in describing another woman. Especially one she remembers from school. *God help you brother, you married a ball buster.*

"I've got to go. Ciao," he says before disconnecting.

Just as well. Having to defend my choices was getting tiresome. I check my watch. Twelve ten. I've been parked here in front of her hotel for half an hour, watching people making their way to the path that leads to the beach. It's a small hotel, but it has the charm of authenticity. This is no tourist trap.

Hope she doesn't overpack. It passes through my mind that all she needs is a bathing suit. Or, maybe not even that. We could hole up in the spa at Sartunia and for the entire time be naked like the statues. I've planned the natural springs for day two. The naked part is her decision. I'm already on board.

Just as my fantasies are taking form, she walks out the front doors. I've made a playlist for our trip. All music from our high school years. Ricky Martin's "Livin la Vida Loca" is playing on my cell, and it's like the opening shot of an epic movie. A fun road trip for old friends or a journey for new lovers? I need to see the entire film to know which.

I get a wave and a smile. Wearing white jeans, sandals, and a marine-blue sleeveless top, she looks so young. She's got the body of a teenager, lean and tight. Tiny but mighty. She only has a small roll-on and her purse. The sunlight on her hair is pretty. It's almost platinum.

"Afternoon! Sorry I'm a little late."

I pop the trunk and get out. We exchange cheek kisses and I take her bag.

"Is this it? Where did you store your other luggage?"

"That's all I need. I can stay for a month with what's in that little thing. Nice Ferrari by the way." She gets in her side.

I shut the trunk and return to my side. Sliding in, I give her a grin. "Are you ready to start our adventure?"

The roar of the engine doesn't drown out her answer. "Hells yeah!" she calls. "Are we winging it, or do you know where we're going?"

"I know. Have you ever been to em—"

She interrupts me with a finger to my lips. "Surprise me," she says.

I nod my agreement and turn the music up as we pull away from the curb. Zarah starts singing along. She knows every word. It's not quite in tune. But it's charming.

I know about every road in and out of Positano. Nona Rosa taught me to drive on these streets. But never have they seemed so vibrant as they do today. Songbirds fly from trees to fountains. The window boxes are packed with flowers, and the colors of the stucco homes and wooden benches lining the cliffs look so rich.

There's an aroma of orange and lemon, mixed with lilac blossoms and freshly baked bread. I may not have paused long enough before to really appreciate what's right here. Or maybe this woman's enhancing all my senses. Sight, smell, hearing, all unexpectedly sharper. That leaves taste and touch. *Gods be kind and let me discover what she can do with those.*

BY THE TIME we're approaching Rome, I'm second-guessing my choice. Not because it wouldn't please her. Hadrian's Villa and Villa d'Este seemed like something she would enjoy. And I could show off a little with my knowledge of the first and fifteenth century palaces and gardens. I'd leave out the fact I learned it all last night when I researched them on the internet.

I thought the Maritime Theater on an island separated by a moat, the bright frescos or the breathtaking gardens of jasmine and cypress trees might be a romantic setting. But there's a flaw in my thinking, and I see it clearly now.

I hired the PhD credentialed docent to give us a private tour. Shit. Talking has been limited by the noise of the Ferrari. We had one loud conversation about our two best friends from high school, Oliver and Stori. They were our idea of a great romance back then.

They had a bad breakup and never saw each other again. Funny, but I still see Oliver in New York and her best friend is still Stori. We made plans to get them back together if we can arrange it.

Mostly we've been singing loudly and laughing about our less-than-perfect voices since Positano. We put memories to each song. Now if we go to the gardens, that'll be another chunk of our limited time together spent not talking. No. I refuse to sabotage my only chance at getting to know her.

Taking the first turnoff, I pull the car into the small clearing next to an empty field and turn the engine off.

"Is this where we're going? You did surprise me," she says with a straight face.

I look into her green eyes with the long eyelashes. They need no makeup to tempt me. And that mouth. I want to know it.

"Whose stupid idea was it to go sightseeing?" I say.

"Yours," she chuckles.

"I want to go to day two's destination. Skip my original plan for today."

"Why? What happened between Positano and Tivoli?" She looks intrigued.

"I realized the greatest adventure for us would be to get to know each other. No marble palace or beautiful garden is going to be as interesting as finding out who we've become."

"You're right." As she says it she's nodding her agreement.

"If I'm being truthful, I want to be alone with you. It's that simple. Am I going too fast, bellezza?"

Her mouth curves into a smile. "We've known each other for twenty years, Fig. Even though most of them we've spent apart. I've decided not to count those."

"Then I'm not counting them either."

"Good. The new plan sounds wonderful. Tell me where we're going," she says.

"Sartunia Hot Springs. They're hidden away in Tuscany. Have you been?"

"No. It'll be a first."

"For both of us then," I say, attempting to rein in my excitement.

"I like that. I don't want to be taken to your go-to seduction site."

I'm taken aback by her comment. "I don't have a go-to seduction site. That's not my style."

"Good answer," she says lifting an eyebrow.

The twinkle in her eyes and the set of her grin gives me ideas. I take her face in my hands and give her a small kiss. We part for just an instant and then it's on. We devour each other. They're real ones this time, nothing veiled in a friendly hello and nothing held back. My pulse quickens with the feel of her tongue. My fingers wrap around the back of her delicate neck, and my lips move to kiss it. She smells like a night-blooming flower. And all I want to do is fuck her. I don't care that I hardly know anything about who she's become. What I see and feel here is enough.

Leaning into my ear she murmurs, "I always wanted you to do that. And more."

My god. Chills.

* * *

I DON'T KNOW if I've ever driven faster. Fifty miles in forty minutes, which is unbelievable for the roads we travel. About mile thirty she put her hand on my neck and ran a finger under my collar as we talked. I got lost in the sensation, and my words came to a halt. I could only concentrate on the sensation.

Now with a few miles to go, I've upped the ante with my hand on her leg. I want to touch her so badly.

In an unbelievably sexy move, she slightly opens her legs then looks up at me with a playfully innocent expression. I'm captivated. She takes my hand and slowly pulls it up her thigh. She's self-assured and strong in such a feminine way, and it's turning me on. She looks like Tinkerbell and thinks like Wonder Woman.

I'd like to rip her clothes off right here. My dick is as hard as an anvil and obvious as hell pushing up against my pants. She reaches over and skims the outline.

"Oh god," I say quietly as I lift my hips toward her hand and just for a moment close my eyes…

HONK!

"Shit!" Zarah screams as we barely avoid being crushed by the truck coming toward us.

I swerve back into my lane. In the heat of the moment I thrusted my arm out trying to protect her, but accidentally bumped hard against her breasts.

"I'm so sorry! Scusami!" I say, pulling over to the side of the road.

Her eyes are wide with fear and her lips are snapped shut. Then we start laughing. It's just a scared chuckle at first, but it builds to an uncontrollable tear-making laugh.

"You almost killed us!"

"That would have really pissed me off," I sigh, leaning my head back against the seat.

"That the last thing you did would be dancing with a semi truck?" She giggles.

"No. That I never got to find out how it feels to be in your bed. I think I could die a happy man after that."

CHAPTER 3

ZARAH

"Signor Dragoni..." is about all I understand. They're talking too fast for my limited command of Italian. But the manager's body language and Fig's obvious pleas not to be cock blocked are clear. The men are the same height, but Fig's body has twice the strength of the skinny man's. Their hands know the same language, gesturing in the air, explaining their sides of the story.

In a final comment, the manager puts his palms together, shakes them and looks heavenward. Fig's wide shoulders drop in defeat.

Turning to me with his mouth set in a hard line, he shakes his head.

"So, I take it we got the Presidential Suite," I tease.

"Not quite. My reservations for two king rooms aren't until tomorrow. The hotel's booked tonight, except for a small room with one double bed. And that won't be vacant and cleaned for another few hours." He looks at his watch. "It's three now. We should just head for the next town. I'm certain I can find something deserving of you."

He sounds so frustrated. So am I.

"Or we could stay here and play it as it comes. I've never slept in a double bed."

The corner of his mouth turns up. "Sleep? I'm not sure either of us are going to get any sleep in any bed in any hotel."

I lean in close to his ear and sigh, "Let's go into the pools then. I don't want to wait any longer. Do you?"

A sound barely heard slips from his lips. It's a half moan.

He turns and takes ahold of my hand. He's talking to the manager again. I'm fairly certain telling him we'll be taking the small accommodations. Meanwhile we'll be in the Hot Springs feeling each other up. Maybe he left that part out.

"Come on. This way," Fig says leading me to the side door.

As we walk out, there's not only the parking lot, but a cobblestone path leading to the front of the hotel. Halfway there I notice the sky is darkening and the wind has whipped up. It lifts a thick piece of his hair and settles it on his forehead. That one out-of-place detail sets me on fire. I stop walking. When he locks eyes with me I see a flash of desire. We go at each other like two horny teenagers.

Taking my hands, he raises them above my head pinning me against the stucco wall. His kisses begin on my lips then move to the neck. Then he starts kissing my breasts and sucking them, right over the silky fabric of my top. I almost melt in a puddle at his feet. God! What a sensation. My nipples pop out in response. I feel the tender bites. For the first time I see the hidden side of Fig. Part animal, all man and absolutely void of shyness when it comes to sex.

My hands are released, and he leans his on either side of me. His forehead rests against mine.

"Touch me." He says it so softly as if it's a prayer.

I wrap one hand gently around his neck and bring my lips to his. Our tongues search for every bit of sexual gratification they can find. Very slowly my other hand trails down the front of his shirt. My fingers dancing across his nipples, over his stomach and to the waistband of his pants. I feel him grow against me as I lay my hand over his impressive package.

"I can't wait," I say against his lips. Tucking my hand inside I touch the head of his cock that lifts for me.

Fig dips his chin and takes in a breath. He pumps for me to go deeper, grab the shaft, do more.

"Take it!" he orders.

Then the door squeaks open and we hear the laughter of two women about to walk outside. Fig and I regain our posture one second after I pull my hand from his pants. Trying to look nonchalant, we start talking just as the two bathers come into view.

"So, we'll change into our swimwear." I may have said that a little too loudly.

"Good," he says looking at my boobs and sending some sort of secret message with his frown, pointed stare and the nod of his head.

I look down at the two wet spots from his sucking fest. My nipples are still erect.

"Oh shit." I cross my arms over the offense just as the women pass.

"Good afternoon," I say looking as guilty as I am.

"Apparently!" the older one answers with a knowing smirk. Her friend let's loose with a loud laugh.

Fig is busy angling his erection away from the bathers' sight line. As soon as they pass and round the corner of the building, we burst out laughing.

"If we get arrested for indecency I'm going to blame you," Fig says trying to tame his stiff cock.

"If we get arrested, you'll be charged with concealing a weapon. A big nightstick," I laugh.

The frown line between his brows softens. "I like how easy it is to be with you. Nothing changes your mood."

"There's nothing at all wrong with today. My mood is because of you."

He looks at me and a smile lights his face. "I feel the same, Zarah."

We walk to the car and he pops the trunk, and we find our swimwear. Mine is three triangles of turquoise, and it fits in my palm. When he eyes it he bites the knuckle of his index finger, which makes me laugh.

"Would you like to change first?" he offers politely.

"I appreciate your being a gentleman," I say smiling. "But wouldn't it be more fun to change together?"

Now he's biting his lip. "That's a much better idea."

Walking toward the changing booths, he takes my hand in his. It feels like the first time a man has ever held my hand.

"They're supposed to be right around the building here," he says.

When we round the corner I'm hit with a breathtaking sight. Wide rushing waterfalls tumble from a dormant volcano high above, into tiered sapphire blue pools. Each can hold at least thirty people comfortably. The top tiers are the most crowded as they're closest to the falls. The bottom few are less popular, and the water is still.

"Isn't it magnificent?"

"All I'm interested in is looking at you," he says.

He grabs the door of a booth just as a man is exiting. "Grazie."

Letting me pass he shuts the door behind him. Music plays over the loudspeakers outside. Lara Fabian sings and it's accompanying our mood. It's a small space with two rusted hooks on the back of the door and a timeworn bench to sit and remove your shoes.

"This was obviously meant for one skinny swimmer. It may be tight," I say with a raised eyebrow.

"I like tight." A muscle in his jaw twitches and then his eyes lower to my body.

"Well then, you're gonna love me," I tease.

His head raises, and we lock eyes.

"I think I always have," he says.

I know he's joking, or caught up in the passion of the moment, but he's not laughing. I decide to ignore his comment because to even entertain the thought he's serious is too crazy.

He faces me without the pretense of looking away and begins to undress. Our bodies so close to each other we're touching. It's possible to move apart a few inches, but why? We go slowly. And we kiss. So many kisses. Deeply, tenderly and for me with an emotion I've never felt before. Passion has been elevated to include a magical state of being. I always thought the idea of falling for someone sounded sort of boring. What a flippin' fool. Nothing routine here.

He unbuttons his shirt. I feel his knuckles against my chest as he undoes each one, down the center where they stop inches away from my pussy. When he opens it I catch myself holding my breath. His chest is hard and golden, stomach flat and toned. Then he takes it off and grabs ahold of my hands and places them both on his beating heart.

I have no smart remarks to make. The man is stealing my words.

He chuckles at my stare. "Let me help you get started," he says, unzipping my pants.

I lift my top over my head and look him in the eye. But it's not my eyes he's gazing at. He runs a finger over the edges of my cups and kisses the flesh that rises with my breath. His hands reach around to the back of my white lacy bra, and he unhooks it. I'm small breasted, but it's kind of a point of pride for me, because they're well shaped and my nipples are prominent and rosy. I know they're hard.

His fingers grasp the shoulder straps and bring the bra down and away.

He looks up into my eyes first, and then directly at my breasts that graze his chest. I hear his intake of breath.

"Bellissimo. Cosi bello, Zarah."

Taking me close with one arm around my waist, his hand finds my nipples. He puts them in his mouth, each one having their turn. Ohhhhhhhh. I feel the hard cock against my belly, pushing, straining to meet me.

"My dick's about to erupt," he says under his breath.

I don't hold back from kissing those lips of his that are so close to mine. Then I purr into his ear. "Unzip. Let me have a preview."

It's just a beat before he looks back into my eyes, smiles, bites his lower lip and unzips. I'm wet with anticipation. He unbuttons the one button holding his pants together. It's almost unbearable feeling him against me as he strips.

"All for you," he says.

I gaze down as he lowers his pants and shorts in one smooth movement. Holy shit. It's a thing of beauty. Rock hard, thick and sized just right for me. I like a challenge. It presses against me, poking my belly.

"Touch me," he commands.

My fingers reach for his cock and encircle the warm masterpiece. Veins run a course around and up to the tip.

"Jesus. Oh God," he gasps looking heavenward.

I bend over as best I can and place my lips on the head. I kiss it. My tongue teases it.

We're interrupted by the banging on the booth door and the Italian voice telling us to hurry things up. I feel Fig's strong hands on my shoulders.

"Let's hurry and get into the water."

He answers the intruder with a sharp retort. I have no idea what was said, but the angry man is silent.

There are no more words exchanged as we continue undressing. It's all visual. He steps out of his pants and his eyes haven't left mine. He smiles as I remove my shoes and pants then do a slow turn so he can check out what's going on behind me. I may have small breasts, but I've got a solid round booty. All my hiking has paid off.

Before I make the complete turn, he spanks my cheek. Then I feel lips kissing away the sting.

"This ass is magnificent," he says holding both arms out and palms up. "I want to worship it."

"Well, let's get in the pools and get to it," I say.

CHAPTER 4

FIG

*Z*arah had to walk in front of me all the way from the booths to the third pool. Hiding my erection was our goal. Although being that close to her perfect ass did nothing to quiet this man's hard on. It was funny because we had to take small unnatural steps to stay close enough. She stopped abruptly to let someone pass, and I smashed right into her. I laughed when she said I could stab somebody with my hard cock.

A light rain has been falling and it's turned the solid path to the pools into a muddy mess. Rocks, twigs, slippery muck make for an interesting walk for the bathers to navigate.

Since we joined them, the crowd has thinned. We're afloat among only thirty or so other bathers in the entire Springs. Only four are in our pool.

It's hard to look away from her graceful form in that blue bikini. And a few minutes back, when she flipped over for the first time and her ass poked out of the water, my dick jumped. What a grand thing it would be to motorboat those apple-shaped cheeks. I'm imagining it now.

Holding up her body as she floats on her stomach, no one can see that my right hand is underwater, inside the bottom of her swimsuit. I'm rubbing her pussy.

The darkened sky can't hold back the torrent any longer and the rain suddenly begins to fall in sheets. Mud along the steep pathway is getting looser and starts a downhill slide. People in every pool move to make their exits. All four of our fellow bathers are climbing out. But not us. Zarah's getting close to coming. I'll stay through a monsoon if need be.

"Holy hell. Don't you stop, Fig," she pleads.

Her ass is rising and falling in tiny pumps, barely visible to anyone but me. It makes little waves in the pool. But with the wind and rain I don't think anyone is able to tell. My middle finger is moving in gentle circles right over her clit, while my dick is begging for relief. I hear the first roll of thunder above me then a shattering crack of lightning. It's followed by Zarah's orgasm.

"Ohhhhhh yeah!" she screams.

Oh, mio dio. Even in this weather I feel a flush creep up my face. More than a few of the people climbing the muddy pathway hear a woman's scream and turn. There's a variety of expressions. Surprise, envy, disgust. One man's laughing and giving me a thumbs up.

She loves a good storm, is all I can think of calling to our uninvited audience.

Zarah takes my hand away and flips over. There's a wide smile on her beautiful face.

"Spectacular! Stupendous!" she says with her version of an Italian accent.

Taking my face in her hands she brings me to her lips. Legs wrap around my waist. I could kiss her for hours if it wasn't that I want to do so much more.

"Senore Dragoni!"

I hear my name called over the rain and wind. The hotel manager is standing at the top of the path, trying to control the umbrella he's holding. He's motioning for us to get out of the pool.

"Maybe our room's ready," Zarah says.

"God, I hope so. Let's go."

We make our way to the edge of the pool. I climb out and extend my hand to lift her.

"Be careful, it's slippery here," I warn.

"Don't worry. I'm good at this kind of thing."

I get her in a standing position. For about two seconds. Her foot slips and she goes backwards. Grabbing my arm for support, we both fall back into the water.

"I'm sorry!" she says with her charming laugh.

I slick back my hair and start laughing. "Let's give it another try."

So we do, and we're successful this time. But it's freezing out of the ninety-nine degree pools. The wind and rain whip our skin, and I see goosebumps spread over her body. Her stupendous nipples could cut glass.

"Take my hand!" I say loudly.

"What?" she says cupping her ear.

I put her hand in mine and hold tight. We start uphill. We're the only people still out here now. Almost every step is a battle. It's a muddy and cold mess of a climb. But with her it feels like one of the best days of my life. We're almost to the top, just three steps away when we slip. We go down hard, and the river of mud takes us back about fifteen feet.

Zarah's laughing so hard tears are welling in her eyes. I start laughing too. Our bodies are covered in mud. Her white hair is caked. She wipes the tears from her cheeks, but all it does is leave a muddy streak across the one place that was still untouched. I laugh.

She picks up a fistful of mud and slings it at me. Landing on top of my head, the pile of goo slides down and onto my chest. I start coming for her. Attempting to avoid me, she only slips and slides further. Her feet and hands are moving, but the rest of her stays in place. I roll on top and easily pin her down. Holding both her hands above her head I gather a handful of mud.

"Don't do it!" she hollers against the rain and wind.

I slowly paint her face with mud. Her neck, her chest. My fingers move under the bikini top and with my mud caked fingers I play with her nipples.

"You bastard!" she says at first, trying to kick her legs. But it only takes one of my thighs to stop that.

Her protest weakens as her nipples respond. I feel her grind and let her roll on top of me. I'm no fool. Now her sweet wet pussy is right atop my dick. That thin strip of fabric barely hides anything. I pull it back and look at her for the first time.

"How beautiful. Like a flower blooming in the mud," I call, running my finger over her lips.

I know she can't hear me, but her hand cups mine and she presses it against her.

"I'm wet," she mouths.

There are rain drops dripping from her hair and face and really every part of her. But I'm certain that's not what she's talking about.

I take ahold of her arms. "Let's quit fucking around. I need to be inside you," I say loud enough for her to hear.

* * *

WE'VE BEEN in this room for two days. Or has it been two hours? No maid service, only food, sleep and conversation interrupted our lovemaking. Even before my dick found its home in her tight pussy I was lost. Once I had a taste of her I was a goner.

I've come to the conclusion that double beds are greatly underrated. Also narrow nondescript showers and windowless boxy rooms with generic bedding. And worn carpets. They're right for making love on when you break the bed frame. We laid the blanket and pillows down and it's made a fine bed.

Something has happened to me in the last forty-eight hours. It's the greatest surprise of my life and without a doubt the most frightening one too.

What if she doesn't feel the same?

Her greatest joy is her independence. What if that requires I let her go?

And as I lay here watching her sleep it strikes me how little I know about the woman. I can't even guess how she'd react if I have the balls to tell her how I feel.

I thought I knew myself. I'm logical and not one to make quick decisions. And yet I can't deny what has happened is unforgettable. It's indelibly written in my soul. But I won't say the words that push to be heard.

Not yet.

Not even to myself.

Awake for an hour, I've been going over the pros and cons. Just like I've done my entire life. Every big decision has been weighed, because I'm not a spur of the moment, fly by the seat of my pants man. Life is too important to be taken lightly. But my chance is now. I may not get another.

My list. So far I have twelve pros and one con. And that one is in some ways a pro. She likes being alone. I do too. But it may be a stronger pull for Zarah. She didn't marry, rarely travels with companions, never yearned for children. Are those choices written in stone? Or are they all because she hasn't met the right man? *Is it me?*

She stirs and the sight of her stretching stops the tape playing in my head.

"Good morning, handsome," she says with the sleepy voice I'm already addicted to.

"It's not a good morning at all," I answer, kissing the top of her head.

"I know."

"Do we have to leave our nest so soon? Is it an absolute necessity you fly back tonight?"

She buries her face against my chest.

"Stay. I don't want you to go," I murmur.

She doesn't say no or yes. She's thinking.

"You should be with me at the wedding. These people are special in my life. Giovanni and Claudia. Come with me please."

The corners of her mouth lift in a little smile. I give it my best shot.

"Plus it's in the Tuscany countryside. The wedding is at their farmhouse. There are beautiful gardens and there's going to be wonderful music and dancing. They're the most interesting couple," I say tracing the shape of her shoulder with my fingers. "Deeply in love at seventy years old. They met in their twenties, but life interrupted their love story. They got another chance though."

"Must have been their destiny." She sighs.

"You'll come with me then?"

She lifts her head and gazes in my eyes. "To paraphrase a line from one of my favorite films, you had me at stay."

CHAPTER 5

ZARAH

"*Y*ou play the violin? I want to hear," I say trailing my fingers over the top of his hand.

"Not anymore. I'm pretty sure Giovanni's ears bled the two years he was giving me lessons."

Driving through the green hills of Tuscany has been awesome. I wouldn't be surprised if heaven turned out looking like this. I'd be okay with that. As long as I could have the same company.

The last half hour has been a tangle of turns. We're going further from the main road as the Ferrari winds up a particularly riotous hill. Everywhere giant sunflowers put on a show, lifting to the sun.

"This is it," Fig says turning onto the gravel road that leads us through two rows of tall skinny cypress trees.

I can tell he's excited to see his friends. When he talked about Giovanni and how close they've been for twenty-five years, it was touching. He spoke of the constant support and interest he felt from the man who taught him the violin. That turned into a real friendship when Fig became a man.

"How old were you when you took lessons?"

He pauses for a few moments then nods his chin. "I think about nine or ten. Look, Zarah!"

Up ahead, nestled in the hillside, sits the sixteenth-century farmhouse. It's like a setting from a movie. Some sort of enchanted dwelling.

As we edge up to the front yard, I see the surrounding silvery olive grove.

"This is magical," I say leaning forward to get a better look.

"I knew you'd find the beauty," he says softly.

He leans over and I get a kiss. And with it an intense look, like he's just realized a great truth.

"What?" I say low.

He snaps out of whatever is holding his attention. With a kind of embarrassment. It's as if I witnessed something I wasn't supposed to.

"No, nothing, nothing. This place! It's fantastico."

He says the words, but I know something powerful just happened. Or is it only wishful thinking on my part? I follow his lead, turn away, and try to distract myself from my own thoughts. Because they're starting to build into a truth I'm not going to be able to ignore much longer. I want him in my life. Permanently.

Anchoring the side of the house is a lush wisteria-draped pergola that runs from corner to corner. And the wide, uncovered, stone floored terrace. A farmhouse dining table, chairs and ottomans await visitors. I imagine unhurried meals spent enjoying good wine and even better friends.

"Oh! There they are!" Fig says bringing the car to a stop, silencing the crackle of gravel under the tires.

Our hosts are coming to greet us, and I hear their muffled voices. One's in Italian, the other in English ... both talking at once. What a stunning couple. They make seventy seem doable. Like there's nothing to fear.

His skin is bronzed from the sun, and a movie star smile and straight white teeth brighten his face. The fact he wears stacked bracelets on one wrist and rolled-up sleeves on his loose white shirt makes him look very cool. The woman is exotically attractive. Wearing a long flowing print dress and earrings that brush her shoulders like a chic hippie. Lovely gray hair falls in waves down her back. They hold hands.

Fig shuts off the engine and we climb out to the open arms of Giovanni and Claudia.

"Figaro!"

Giovanni greets his friend with glistening eyes. And when I glance at Fig, his are shimmering with tears too.

"You're the first ones here!" Claudia says.

The two men hug and kiss each other's cheek with ease. They don't let go quickly. There's none of the embarrassment of affection I see so often in other cultures, including my own.

Fig turns and holds out his hand to me as I walk around the car and join them.

"And who is this beautiful girl?" Giovanni says, eyes twinkling.

Fig beams. "This is Zarah…. Zarah I'd like you to meet my dear friends Giovanni and Claudia. The happy bride and groom."

"We're glad you'll be joining us, Zarah! It's just wonderful!" Claudia says enfolding me in an embrace.

She smells like an exotic flower.

"Thank you. Your property is stunning."

Giovanni reaches for me. "Don't forget Giovanni. I want a hug too."

"Welcome to Nido d'Amorre. You know what that translates to?"

"I'm afraid my Italian isn't very good. But I did get the *Love* part."

"The Love Nest. Maybe it will be that for you."

Fig and I exchange glances. He's nibbling on his bottom lip and I'm grinning like an embarrassed schoolgirl.

* * *

WE'RE A SMALL GROUP, maybe twenty-five. The stars shine brightly in the black sky, and an atmosphere of love hangs heavy in the air. To be among such happy people for two days has been a gift. Everyone here is sharing in the joy of the union that just took place under the full moon, next to the wisteria-draped pergola.

Now we sit at the long farmhouse table enjoying the last of an indescribable Italian feast, and one of many glasses of champagne.

Giovanni plays the final notes of the violin solo he performed for his bride. There's not a dry eye as the applause and whistles sound. All the feeling he has for her was said in one heartfelt instrumental. They embrace.

Setting down his instrument, our attention is pulled by the clinking of Claudia's knife on her champagne flute as she stands and looks in the eyes of her beloved.

"My love. I want to tell our story to our dearest friends." She turns to the guests. "For those who don't know, Giovanni and I first met in nineteen sixty-seven. I was an eighteen-year-old tourist backpacking through Italy. He was a twenty-one-year-old violinist working on the score to Fellini's "Romeo and Juliet" in a studio in Rome."

The guests are smiling, and Fig just squeezed my hand when he gazed at my face.

"We met in a café and within a couple of days we fell in love. True love. We were inseparable for the three weeks. Although we spent our time mostly in bed!" Everyone chuckles. "I'm certain it was love even then. But we were young, and in the eternal city where fairy tales happen regularly. He wanted me to stay. I doubted my own heart. After all, I had just begun my life plan. I'd travel the world while I was young. It would be glorious."

She pauses and looks to her left and right, into the faces of the guests.

"And it was. I got my dream. I saw the world. But all along the way, I thought of what I had left behind."

She takes Giovanni's chin in her hand.

"What I didn't know then, and for many years after, was all along the world existed right here."

Giovanni kisses her hand, and tears shine in both their eyes.

"So I raise my glass to you, my darling. Knowing never again will I travel any other world."

Giovanni stands and takes her in a tight embrace. My hand covers my mouth and the sobs that want to escape. Fig is wiping tears from his cheeks. We're not alone.

"I have just one thing to say," Giovanni announces. He looks into his bride's eyes. "We're together. I forget the rest," he says waving the very idea away.

They kiss. Whistles and applause. The music starts.

* * *

FOUR HOURS LATER, Fig and I are still dancing. But now we're alone under the stars and it's a new day. The guests have trickled away; the bride and groom have gone to their marriage bed. Mostly we sway, holding tightly to each other. My head rests on his chest, and he's holding my right hand over his heart. Funny how every song tonight was about us. This one, Il Volo's, "I Can't Help Falling In Love", especially.

His lips touch the shell of my ear. "Some things are meant to be," he whispers.

My heart skips a beat with the thought he may be feeling what I am. I look into his eyes.

"I believe that too."

Our dancing slows to a stop. But in its place I feel like every cell in my body is being reborn.

"I love you," he says clear and certain.

This moment. This is the one I'd choose to relive over and over if ever a god asks.

And then I say the truest thing I've ever said. "I love you too, Fig. I do without a doubt."

His expression reflects mine. Pure untethered joy. And with it comes happy tears.

"You've made a believer of me. It's you. Now I know it always has been," he says.

Nestling my face against his chest, I kiss the place over his heart. I feel his strong hands on my shoulders. Then he lifts my chin and looks into my eyes.

"Beautiful girl with the silver hair, I want to go with you on the greatest adventure of our lives. Will you marry me, Zarah?"

My body is tingling. My face feels the flush rise. And my heart. My heart.

I lift my arms around his neck and thread my fingers through his hair. Right before I kiss him, I smile.

"Yes. A thousand times yes. I guess I always wanted you to do that."

ABOUT THE AUTHOR

USA TODAY bestselling author, Leslie Pike, has loved expressing herself through the written word since she was a child. Her passion for film and screenwriting led her to Texas for eight years, writing for a prime time CBS series. Leslie lives in Southern California with her Pom-Poo, Mr. Big. She's traveled the world as part of film crews, from Africa to Israel, New York to San Francisco. Now she finds her favorite creative adventures taking place in her home, writing Contemporary Romance.

Connect With Leslie
www.lesliepike.com
Facebook Readers Group: Leslie's Ladies

ACKNOWLEDGMENTS

Writing seems like a solitary art, but that's not strictly true. There are silent partners in my vision, helpers in league with the dreamer. Invisible hands lifting so I can have a better view of myself. Sharp eyes reading every story told. There are shoulders to stand on so I can see what's possible, letting me know what to aim for. So to all the good-hearted companions in the dream, I say thank you, with an undeniable feeling of gratitude.

Nichole Strauss, Insight Editing Services
Kari March, Kari March Designs

Printed in Great Britain
by Amazon

28784448R00025